Indonesian Tales
of Treasures and Brides

Told and Edited by Kuniko Sugiura

Illustrated by Koji Honda
Translated by Matthew Galgani
Executive Editor: Miyoko Matsutani

HEIAN

Hearing Tales as They Are Told

Do you love to listen to stories? I do. Can you listen really well?

For hundreds of years, people have passed down folktales from grandparents and parents to children by telling—not writing—them.

When people tell you a story, you don't just hear with your ears. You learn a lot from the voices the storytellers use, how they move their arms, legs, head, shoulders, and body, the expressions on their face—all the tools they use to make their tales come alive.

This book, and the others in the series Asian Folktales Retold, was created to help you truly "hear" Asian folktales and understand them deeply.

As you listen to these tales, or perhaps read them yourself when you're older, figure out for yourself what they mean. If you can hear the storyteller's voice in your head, then you are listening really well.

Published by HEIAN, P.O. Box 8208, Berkeley, California 94707
HEIAN is an imprint of Stone Bridge Press
www.stonebridge.com • sbp@stonebridge.com

LIBRARY OF CONGRESS CATALOGING-IN-PUBLICATION DATA

Sugiura, Kuniko, 1943–
    [Katari obasan no Indonesia minwa. English. Selections]
    Indonesian tales of treasures and brides / told and edited by Kuniko Sugiura;
illustrated by Koji Honda; translated by Matthew Galgani; executive editor Miyoko
Matsutani.
        v. cm.—(Asian folktales retold)
    "Originally published in Japan by Hoshinowakai"—Copyright p.
    Summary: Three Indonesian folktales, one of a man who happily marries a goddess
but cannot keep a promise he made her, one of a man who gives all he has to win the
hand of a princess, and one of two stepsisters whose different natures bring each her
proper reward.
    Contents: The goddess-bride—The best gift of all—The pumpkin treasure.
    ISBN-13: 978-0-89346-951-1 (hardcover)
    1. Tales—Indonesia. [1. Folklore—Indonesia.] I. Honda, Koji, 1962– ill. II.
Galgani, Matthew. III. Matsutani, Miyoko, 1926– IV. Title.
    PZ8.1.S943Ind 2007
    398.2—dc22
    [E]
                                                        2006033772

The Goddess-Bride

Long, long ago, there was a lake whose
surface was as calm and smooth as the glass
of a mirror. The water was so clear that
you could see right to the bottom. Flowers
bloomed on the shore all around. You could
watch reflections of the clouds move across
this very beautiful lake. You could even see
the distant mountains where the gods were
said to live. It was a truly amazing place.

In the village nearby lived a young
man who loved this lake a great deal. To
keep the water pure and clear, he made sure
that beautiful flowers with lovely aromas
bloomed around it at all times.

But one morning, when he arrived to care for the lake, he was shocked to find the water muddy.

"That's strange," the young man thought. "There haven't been any rainstorms or heavy winds."

The next morning, again, the lake was muddy. And plucked flowers were scattered all along the shore. Upset and angry, the young man stayed up all the next night, watching the lake, waiting to catch whoever was doing such harm.

That night there happened to be a full moon. As the young man enjoyed the beautiful moonlight, he saw some birds flying down to the lake from the sky. There were seven in all.

"What kind of bird would be flying in the middle of the night?" he wondered as he watched them. Then he saw that they weren't birds at all. They were goddesses from the heavens, approaching the lake, their clothes flowing behind them in the wind. When they arrived, they removed their dresses and began bathing in the water in their underclothes.

Now, Indonesian people love bathing—they call it "mandi"—and these goddesses were no different. They were having a wonderful time in the lake.

The young man was surprised to see this, as he watched from behind a tree. All of the goddesses were incredibly pretty, but the youngest one was particularly beautiful.

Seeing that the goddesses had left their dresses on the shore, the young man quietly took the dress of the youngest goddess and ran off to hide it in the storehouse where he kept his rice. Then he went back to watching the goddesses bathe.

As they bathed, the goddesses laughed and played, taking turns plucking flowers and putting them in one another's hair. When they prepared to return home, they discovered that the dress of the youngest goddess had disappeared. She looked everywhere for her dress, while the others got dressed. Then they all helped her search, but her dress was nowhere to be found.

"We're out of time,"
the other goddesses said.
"We have to go home right
away. You'll have to stay and
look for your dress yourself
and catch up with us later."
With that, they flew back to
the heavens.

Sad and all alone, the
youngest goddess began to
cry. Just then, the young
man called out to her.

"What are you doing in
a place like this at this time
of night?" he asked.

Startled, the young
goddess turned toward
the young man, but as she
was clothed only in her
underwear, she was too
embarrassed to answer.

"If you don't have any
clothes," the young man
said, "I can offer you this
sarong." And he handed her
a length of cloth.

You see, in Indonesia, people take a piece of cloth called a sarong and wrap it very skillfully around themselves to make a skirt. The goddess wrapped the sarong around herself just as an Indonesian girl would.

"Come to my house," the young man said. "I can give you food and clothes that will fit you perfectly." The young man took her hand and led the goddess to his home.

The beautiful goddess stayed at the young man's house, and in time they were married. Soon a beautiful baby boy was born to them.

The goddess, who was now a wife and mother, worked hard to keep their house spotless, making the young man very happy. But there was one strange thing about their household: Even though they ate rice every day, they never ran out of rice. In fact, the amount of rice in the young man's storehouse never changed at all. And whenever the goddess-bride was preparing the rice, she forbade anyone to enter the kitchen.

One day, the goddess-bride had to go to the river to do the laundry. She had been cooking rice, and she said to her husband, "Please watch the fire until I get back. But don't, for any reason, open the lid and look at what's inside the pot."

"All right, I won't look," her husband promised.

But, as soon as she left, he thought, "Here's my chance to discover her secret about the rice." And he slowly lifted the lid to look inside the pot.

What do you think he saw? There was only a single grain of rice inside!

"Wow!" the young man exclaimed, quite impressed. "With her

magical powers, my goddess-bride can make a pot of rice from a single grain! That's why we never run out of rice." Very carefully, he closed the lid and pretended he hadn't looked inside.

A little while later, the goddess-bride returned and looked inside the pot. She sighed sorrowfully and then said to her husband, "You opened the lid. You did the one thing I asked you not to do."

"If my powers are seen by a mortal being like you," she explained sadly, "then they disappear."

Now that her powers were gone, the young goddess-bride had to wake up early each morning to clean the rice. That meant, of course, that she had to bring rice in from the storehouse, and the supply of rice there quickly got smaller. In  time, she reached the very bottom of the pile, and what do you think she found? Of course, her dress! That was where the young man had hidden it on the night he first saw her.

When she discovered the dress, she suddenly recalled all her memories of her past life, and she wanted desperately to return to her home in the heavens.

"I'm going back," she said to her husband. "But I can't bring our child, because he was born here on earth. Please be sure to love him and raise him well. Promise me you'll do that."

"Wait," her husband begged. "Please, don't go! I won't know what to do without you. And our son—think how sad he'll be without his mother."

The young man pleaded desperately with his wife, scared and shocked that he might lose her.

"Whenever you feel that you must see me," she replied calmly, "look up at the moon when it is full. You will see my reflection there." And with that, the goddess put on her dress and rode the wind back to her home in the heavens.

From that day on, on the night of every full moon, the young man and his son would stare into the sky, comforted by the kind face of the goddess reflected in the moon.

And that's the end of the story of the young man who couldn't keep a promise when told not to peek.

The Best Gift of All

Long, long ago, on a faraway island, there lived a king who had a very beautiful daughter. Not only was she lovely to look at, but she was also beloved because she was so kind and so smart. As you might guess, then, a huge number of suitors came asking for her hand in marriage.

The king adored his
daughter, so he wanted
to be sure that she didn't
marry the wrong man.
After thinking a good deal,
he announced:

"Anyone who wishes
to marry the princess must
bring a gift that proves
how much he loves her and
how happy he will make her
in marriage. The princess, not I, will be the
judge of the gifts. The man whose gift most
appeals to the princess's heart shall take
her as his bride."

The king then chose the day and
place for suitors to present their gifts.
His proclamation spread all through
the country and neighboring lands.
Princes, noblemen, and wealthy
suitors from near and far came to
compete. Every man searched high
and low for a grand and expensive gift
that would win the princess's heart.

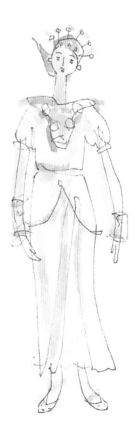

Now, at this time, in a small, remote village, a poor young man named Takatorian lived with his mother.

The king's proclamation reached even Takatorian's village. And Takatorian, too, wanted to give the princess an offering that would win her heart. He thought for days about what he might give her. Then, suddenly, he decided. He went into the forest, and he did not return even when night fell. The next day and the day after that he still did not come home.

His worried mother packed food and drink and headed out to look for him. She found him beside the best tree in the forest, which he had just chopped down. Takatorian was earnestly carving something from its wood.

As she wiped the sweat from his brow, his mother asked, "What are you working so hard on?"

At first, Takatorian said nothing, but when he saw the worried look on his mother's face, he replied. "It's my gift for the princess."

His mother was taken aback. "You? A gift for the princess?" she exclaimed. "The princess won't accept a gift from a man who has no money. She'll only laugh at you. Stop this foolishness this instant!"

But Takatorian simply said, "Mother, I'm making a doll in the image of the kindest, smartest, and most wonderful woman in the world. If I build it well, I want the princess to see it. Of course, I've never seen her, so I'm just imagining what such a woman might look like."

Takatorian blushed a little as he spoke. Seeing his face, his mother fell silent. She left the food and drink for him and returned home, praying with all her might for the gods to protect her son and give him strength.

Many days later, the doll was finished at last. It was incredibly beautiful, with the smoothest of skin. But Takatorian was still not satisfied. So he cut his own hair, dyed it a pretty color, and one by one, attached the strands to the doll's head. Next he put makeup on her face, and used lovely flower buds as the pupils for her eyes. The doll now looked as if it actually had a soul.

But how should he dress the doll? Takatorian was stumped.

Then his mother said, "What about this?" and offered him a piece of beautiful material. Handed down from his father, who had passed away, it was a luxurious cloth with an exquisite intricate design.

"Your father will certainly be watching over you now," said his mother.

"Thank you, Mother," said Takatorian, and he went right to work sewing the clothes for his precious doll.

At long last, the day came for the princess to receive the gifts
from her suitors. The king and the princess sat waiting in the palace
as magnificent and famous suitors gathered, each confident in the gift
he had brought. Dressed in his humble and ragged clothes, Takatorian
waited at the back of the line, holding his wooden doll.

One prince presented the princess with an ivory comb studded
with diamonds.

"My fine prince," the princess said in a beautiful voice, "surely
there is not another comb in the world that could compare to this."

"Not so, Princess," said the prince proudly. "If you come to my
country, you shall have countless combs like this one."

One nobleman offered the princess a necklace made of the largest pearls you've ever seen.

"This must be one-of-a-kind," she marveled. "I'm sure these pearls are extremely rare."

"Not so, Princess," said the nobleman. "Marry me, and you shall have many more."

Next, a very wealthy merchant presented the finest silk cloth.

"This is extraordinary silk," said the princess. "Where did you find it?"

"From a faraway land," the merchant replied, his chest puffed out with pride. "In my dresser, you will find nothing but the finest materials from all over the world."

And so it went, with suitor after suitor presenting the princess with the finest, most expensive items money could buy.

Then, when all the other suitors were done, it was Takatorian's turn to offer his gift.

"That's a lovely doll," said the princess. "Do you have many such dolls?"

"No," replied Takatorian, looking straight into the princess's eyes. "Just this one. I put all my energy into this work, carving my image of the ideal woman. So this is the only one I have."

The princess, who had been gazing into the eyes of the doll, looked up and smiled at Takatorian.

Then the king spoke. "My daughter, whose present do you choose?"

"I choose Takatorian's gift," answered the princess. "I believe his is the most precious."

When the other suitors heard this, they were astonished and angry. How could the princess choose a handmade wooden doll over the rare and extremely expensive presents they had offered? "We've been taken for fools!" they shouted.

But the king responded, "All of you offered just one of the many things you own. And you boasted of all the other wealth you possess. Takatorian, on the other hand, offered everything he had to give, a true sign of his love. I stand by my daughter's decision."

On hearing the king's rebuke, the suitors hung their heads in shame and left the palace sadly.

Soon, Takatorian and the princess were married. Together they helped their country flourish, and they lived happily ever after.

And that is the end of the story of the young man who poured his whole heart into a gift and won the heart of a princess.

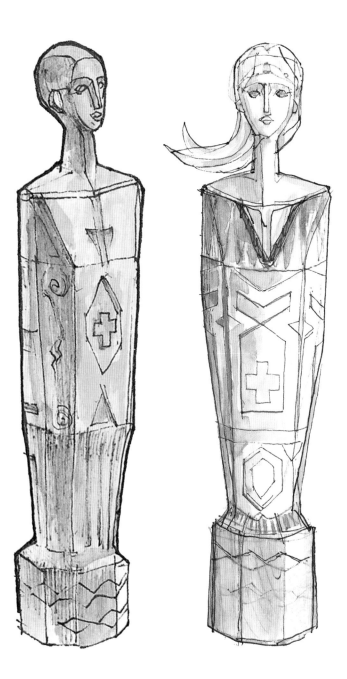

The Pumpkin Treasure

There's a type of onion called "bawan" in Indonesia. "Merah" means red, so "bawan merah" means red onion—a very small onion. "Putih" means white, so you might think "bawan putih" would mean white onion, right? But it doesn't! It actually means garlic. Of course, both are important ingredients for cooking. This story is about two stepsisters who had the names Bawan Merah and Bawan Putih.

Once upon a time, a girl named Bawan Putih lived happily with her mother and father. Then, one day, her mother suddenly fell ill and died. Bawan Putih was grief-stricken and, from that day on, did nothing but weep. Seeing how sad she was, her father thought that she needed a new mother who would love and care for her, so he decided to find a new wife.

What a surprise! Bawan Putih's new stepmother had a daughter named Bawan Merah, and Bawan Putih was filled with joy to have a sister.

At first, Bawan Putih's stepmother gave both girls the same love and care, but after a while she became mean and unkind to her stepdaughter. She made Bawan Putih do all the chores. From early morning until late at night, Bawan Putih had to wash the clothes, clean the dishes, and scrub the floors. By bedtime, she was completely exhausted. Sometimes, if she dropped and broke a dish because she was so tired, her stepmother would get angry and beat her.

One day when Bawan Putih
was washing clothes in the
river, Bawan Merah's clothes
were swept away in the
current.

"What am I going to
do now?" Bawan Putih cried.
"How can I tell my stepmother
that I lost Bawan Merah's
clothes? She'll be furious!" So she
started running after the clothes. But the river current was fast, and the
clothes soon floated away out of sight.

Bawan Putih headed downriver after them, and, in a while, she
met a cattle farmer.

"Mr. Cattle Farmer," she called, "have you see any clothes float by
here?"

"Yes, I have," the farmer replied. "But they've already gone
downstream."

So Bawan Putih headed farther down the river. In a while, she met
a horse rancher.

"Mr. Horse Rancher," she called, "have
you seen any clothes float by here?"

"Yes, I have," the horse rancher
replied. "But they've already gone
downstream. Try the old woman
down there. She might know
where they are."

"Thank you," said
Bawan Putih, and she headed
downstream.

After running a long time, she came upon an old house where an old woman was standing in the doorway.

"Old Woman," Bawan Putih said, "have you see any clothes float by here?"

"Yes, I have," the old woman replied. "I gathered them up and have them here. I was waiting for someone to come looking for them."

"Thank you, thank you!" cried Bawan Putih, full of excitement. "They floated away while I was washing them. May I have them back, please?"

"Of course," said the old woman. "But first I need you to help me with my work."

The old woman was holding a basket of rice, so Bawan Putih quickly strained and cleaned the rice. Then she followed the old woman into her house.

It felt very strange and eerie inside. The old woman's bowls and utensils were made from the bones of some kind of animal, and a human skull was sitting on top of the kitchen table. But Bawan Putih somehow found the courage to clean the rooms and help prepare a meal for the two of them. The old woman seemed very pleased with Bawan Putih's efforts. The meal was delicious, and, once her stomach was full, Bawan Putih regained her strength.

"I'd like to go home now," Bawan Putih said.

After returning the clothes, the old woman announced, "Because you worked so hard, I want to give you this as your reward." She handed Bawan Putih a pumpkin, but she warned, "Now, don't cut it open until you get all the way home."

When Bawan Putih got home, she sliced open the pumpkin. What a surprise! It was filled with gold, precious gems, and money!

Bawan Putih told her stepmother everything that had happened. But her stepmother said, "Since it was Bawan Merah's clothes that you were looking for, this reward belongs to her." And with that, the stepmother took all the treasure.

Even that wasn't enough for the greedy stepmother. She wanted more treasure, so she told Bawan Merah to do what Bawan Putih had done.

Bawan Merah went down to the river, but, instead of even pretending to wash her clothes, she just threw them into the current, and then chased after them.

In a while, she met the cattle farmer. But she went right past him without even a greeting.

A little while later, she met the horse rancher and went right past him, too, as if he weren't even there.

Then she came upon the old woman standing in front of her house.

"Old Woman," said Bawan Merah. "Some clothes floated down here, didn't they? Well, they're mine, so give them back."

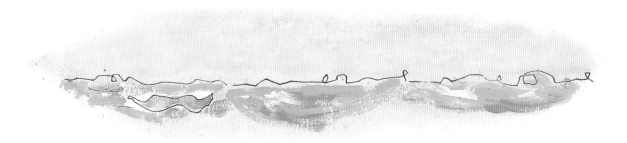

The old woman stared at Bawan Merah and then said, "Oh, I'll give them back to you. But first I need you to help me with my work."

Bawan Merah was in no mood for housework. However, she wanted the reward, so she followed the old woman into the house. She swept a little here and there, and she splashed some water on the dishes. Then she just stood around impatiently.

The old woman had had enough. "It's time for you to go," she said, and handed Bawan Merah her clothes. But Bawan Merah just stood there in a huff.

"So you want a pumpkin, too, eh?" asked the old woman. "I'll give you one. But don't cut it open until you get all the way home."

"At last! I've got the pumpkin," thought Bawan Merah, and she hurried out the door. But she couldn't stop wondering what treasures it held. She just had to know right away. So she decided to cut it open.

Well, what do you think happened? I bet you've guessed that what came out of the pumpkin wasn't gold, precious gems, or money. It was disgusting bugs and dangerous insects. They stung and bit Bawan Merah until she ran away screaming and crying. In fact, she never came home.

Her worried mother went looking for her, but, alas, she never found Bawan Merah.

So the treasure Bawan Putih had earned from the old woman became her own once again. And she lived happily ever after.

And that's the end of the story of the stepsisters Bawan Putih and Bawan Merah and their pumpkins.

About the Series and This Book

The Asian Folktales Retold series was created to capture the spirit of Asian folktales and give them new life, showing children how these stories help us both evaluate the modern world and connect with a rich cultural past. The stories strive to preserve the oral flavor of recountings of tales passed down for generations, and they are intended to be read aloud to experience the full joy of this picture book.

Like all folktales, the stories in this book have been passed down verbally, but because Indonesia is peopled by so many ethnic groups, they were told in different languages and versions in different regions. This book gathers highly popular stories that a visitor living in Jakarta for just a few years would come to know.

About the Storyteller and Editor

When Kuniko Sugiura was born, in 1943 in Aichi Prefecture, Japan, her father was in Indonesia, and she developed a lifelong love for and interest in that country. Sugiura graduated from Aichi Prefectural University and became involved in telling folktales through her work with children's books.

Sugiura's granddaughter was 20 months old when the author's son-in-law was transferred to a job in Indonesia, and his family moved there. Sugiura loved singing lullabies, reciting nursery rhymes, and telling fairy tales to her grandchild in Japanese, but when she visited the family in Indonesia she developed an interest in sharing Indonesian folktales with the child, too. She asked her daughter for the Indonesian stories children liked best and told those to her granddaughter. She also turned to Internet sources and print collections for Indonesian folklore.

After studying folktales in the course of her travels, Sugiura researched how these stories are currently told and experienced. She has written and edited several Japanese-language books on folklore and storytelling and is an active member of many folklore associations.

About the Illustrator

Born in 1962 in Ishikawa Prefecture, Japan, artist Koji Honda graduated with a degree in sculpture from the Kanazawa College of Art. From 1985 to 1993, he worked at Maeda Outdoor Arts Design, designing monuments, sculptures, and other works. In 1997, he illustrated and oversaw the design of the five-volume series Biotope de Asobo (Having Fun with Biotope), published by Hoshinowakai. Since 1999, Honda's artworks have been included in several exhibitions.

About Indonesia

Indonesia is made up of almost 18,000 islands. Some are very large, like Java, Sumatra, and Borneo, but many others are tiny, and more than 7,000 are uninhabited. The islands stretch about 3,000 miles from east to west, forming the world's largest archipelago nation.

Most of the country is in the southern hemisphere, but part crosses the equator and extends into the northern hemisphere. The population is more than 200 million and includes 250 to 300 ethnic groups, who speak more than 300 languages.

From infancy, babies hear and learn a native ethnic language. Once in school, children learn to speak Indonesian, the common language that the people use to communicate across ethnic groups.

Indonesia's people vary widely in the way they look—with a range of skin colors, eye shapes, and hair colors and textures. While the majority of Indonesians are Muslim, a variety of religions and ways of thinking are found among the islands' peoples.

Each ethnic group has its unique customs and culture, passed down from the days long before Indonesia was unified as a country. One important way traditions pass from generation to generation is in folktales.

Other Books from Heian

Asian Folktales Retold

VIETNAM

Told and Edited by Masao Sakairi

Illustrated by Shoko Kojima

Vietnamese Fables of Frogs and Toads

The Frog Bride, The Toad Who Brought the Rain

ISBN-13: 978-0-89346-947-4

Vietnamese Tales of Rabbits and Watermelons

The Rabbit Who Always Got Away, Mai An-Tiem and the Watermelons

ISBN-13: 978-0-89346-948-1

CHINA

Told by Miwa Kurita

Illustrated by Saoko Mitsukuri

China Tells How the World Began!

How the World Began, Why Cats Hate Rats

ISBN-13: 978-0-89346-944-3

Chinese Fables Remembered

The Brothers and the Birds, The Two Rooster Friends

ISBN-13: 978-0-89346-945-0

Each volume $16.95, hardcover